6
FEET
DEEP
IN
THOUGHT

———

POEMS

MCKAY TK CHILD

© 2023, Text by McKay Child
©2023, Cover art by McKay Child

All rights reserved. No parts of this publication may be reproduced in any form without the prior written permission of the author.

ISBN: 9798390913420

*For those whom these poems are about,
but will never read them.*

A deep love and thanks to all the friends and poets who helped with and inspired me; to L who put up with my incessant ramblings while writing; to my editor and sister Jerusha Smith, without whom I would be lost; and to my dog, Bone, who would give me a gentle nudge when I needed a break from myself.

CONTENTS

Love, Lament, and Loss………………..……..……. .P. 3
   Poems 1-46

Hatred, Isolation, and Disgust………………....…P. 77
   Poems 47-96

Unseen Horrors and Unknown Realities………...P. 157
   Poems 97-117

PREFACE

My love for poetry was ingrained in me at a young age with the likes of Shel Silverstein, Carol Lynn Pearson, and the hopelessly romantic lyrics of 80's love ballads, although, up until a few years ago, I never considered writing any of my own.

At the beginning there was a smattering of words about love and heartache, but I found myself beginning to delve deeper into emotions of loss and depression I hadn't had a way to process before. As the pages became a substantial stack, this project became a much-needed catharsis for my mental health.

The three sections of this book seemed necessary to contain the overlying themes in these poems. "Love, Lament, and Loss" is an outpouring of emotion for other people I am either close to, or no longer able to be close to. "Unseen Horrors and Unknown Realities" holds stories of abstract confusion, murder, and nightmarish dreamscapes. The most difficult for me was the contents of "Hatred, Isolation, and Disgust", where I visit my feelings on religion, depression, and suicidal ideation. I spent countless hours researching places, methods, and people related to suicide; I found myself pouring over endless pages of suicide notes, and even wrote a few of my own.

I honestly can't say for sure if forcing myself into a mindset I've already been in most of my life has been "healing," but it certainly has been an eye-opening journey of becoming intimate with an illness so many of us live with, yet hardly know.

I chose to surround these sections with quotes from Fyodor Dostoevsky, as his writing has always been a comfort for me, and his romantic existentialism fully encompasses the atmosphere of this body of work.

Please reach out when you need lifting up, because you are not alone.

-McKay Child

> "*At this moment, a thousand valves have opened within my brain, and I must pour forth a river of words or I shall suffocate.*"
>
> \- Fyodor Dostoevsky

Love,
Lament,
And
Loss

*"To love is to suffer
and there can be no love
otherwise."*

-Fyodor Dostoevsky

1.

She came
Along
And he found himself.

But
He became
Lost
In her.

There were no grand
Gestures.
No
Noticeable
Sway...
Or
Notable
Shift.

Just
Her
Quiet chaos,
Embracing
His
Deafening calm.

2.

I've known you for so long.
You snuck out of the house and we met in the rain;
Droplets leaving wet trails down the wall
Underneath my window we forgot to close.
Trying to be silent but
Forgetting anything
And anyone else who might hear.

But
Passion
Has turned into
Lament.

That time under the willow,
Unseen and warm in the throws of
Summer sun
And
Spring flowers,
When I was certain
I had known you
Over infinite lifetimes,
And you told me you'd
Found me again.

But now I'm searching,
And I'm not sure what a
Lifetime is,
Much less how many I can handle.

A mountain of letters with your name and
Scent;
It smells like
Youth and regret.

Small talk formed in ink,
Nothing immortalized is more significant
Than something forgotten.

And here I am..
Still existing
Without you,
My body filled with
Feathers and scales.
I know you would love that.

Here I am..
Forced to spend years
Remembering you,
And the short moments I had with you.
Before you were filled
With the chemical nothing
And a blind lover.
Blood on your knuckles;
Delicate,
Broken,
And worth nothing.

All color is dimmed;
My teeth are filled with grit,
And I chew on the stones
Of uncontrollable passings
And
Unrealized rapture.

3.

Standing here
Amongst the
Nettle and sunflower,
The wind
Ever so slightly
Moves your hair
Across your face,
In a brush stroke
Of
Cinnamon.

Your shawl falls to the side
And
Your shoulder is laid bare,
Exposing the
Irresistible sensuality
Of your neck
To
The sunlight.

These
Are the moments
That
My mind quiets
And I forget
The chaos of existence.

These
Are the moments
That keep me alive.

4.

I used to worry
That I wouldn't be able to
Find someone like you
Again;

In the end,
I'm pretty sure that's
A
Good thing.

5.

Long walks
Your head in the air
Or
Nose to the ground,
Catching a glimpse of
Some other place
Or time.
A heavy flop
Onto cool grass
And
Legs to the sky
Basking in
Sunshine and belly rubs.

Your muzzle grows gray,
Our walks grow shorter...
And
I hold tight to you at night,
For fear that
No one else will remind me
To
Appreciate warm sun
And cool grass
Ever again.

6.

If you were the ocean,
I would stray off course,
Lost in the crashing blue.

If you were a flame,
You would burn through the night,
Rekindled upon waking
To chase the darkness
To
Dusty corners.

If you were morning,
You'd be the warm flush of sunrise
Dancing through the pane.

If you were a forest,
You would be beautiful and vast,
Blossoming with green,
And pathless;
Unknown mysteries to be uncovered.

If you were the wind,
You would lift up fallen feathers
And carry the heavens on your back,
Powerful and effortless.

If you were the sky,
You would move in an unending
Choreograph of planets and cosmos,
And I would lay awake to
Ponder your stars.

If you were the earth,

I would run barefoot and free
Through your clovered meadows,
And marvel
At your honest grandeur.

If you were a stone,
You would stand stoic,
Diamonds tossed aside
In mines committed to your discovery.

If you were a rope,
I would not make it to another dawn;
Entangled and breathless,
Offering up all that I have
To feel your lips upon my neck.

7.

You are in the
Golden hour of your life,
Who am I to
Shade the sun
From
Lighting on your skin
As you blossom,
Discovering yourself
And
Your place in this world?

8.

It seems
That everyone
Has some story
About
"The one that got away".

How strange
We frame
Our own failures
As someone leaving us,
When in fact
We let them go
Unappreciated
And
Undervalued
For so long,

Until
They finally sink to the earth
And watch as we
Move on
Never looking back
Until the time for
Repentance
Has passed.

Humans do not exist,
Just
Penitent monsters
Every last one of us.

I don't have
One that got away,

Just several
That
I allowed to die.

9.

Sometimes
When you got up
Before me,
I would move over to
The feminine hollow
Left on your side
Of the bed,
And try to fit myself
Into the
Warmth of it;

Now
In a different city,
In a different home,
In a different bed,
I find myself still trying…
Trying to
Fit myself
Into a
You shaped
Embrace
I know isn't there.

10.

All I want
Is to sleep;
Dreamless,
And numb.

Yet I lie awake,
Sometimes because of
The immense weight
Of
Overlapping thoughts
And guilt,
And
Sometimes
No thoughts at all.

All I want
Is to sleep
For years,
Never waking
Until
When I do
You are there beside me
Again.

11.

His heart was shattered
From the moment he saw her.

The panicked
Claustrophobic knowledge
Of a life wasted
Loving anyone else...
Until now.

Endless hours.
Infinite time.
Throat raw;

The bloody cough
Of every combination of words
Could never be enough.

Stifled lungs;
A persistent gasp.
Stomach turned
To wet leather.
Bones
Aching
To break free
And
Feel
Her.

An intense
Agony
Of unrealized
Desire.

Her heart swelled
From the moment she saw him.

"I don't want to hurt you..."
She whispered.

12.

She was
Brilliantly aflame -
A
Pillar of chaos
Lit on fire,
Hands crusted in
Ache
And
Mouth full of
Grace.

She was the
Arms and teeth
Of
Insecurity.
The
Tongue and feet
Of
Judgement,
Blinded by the years of
Eyes kept fearfully peeled,
And
Face stained with salt.

She had fed her warmth
Until it was a
Forest in flames,
An
Uncontrollable inferno,
All consuming
And
Raging;

So she dug a

Lonely pit,
Put herself out
Within it,
And lay there
Smoldering.

She waited
For eternity,
In silent hope
That someone would
Come along
And bathe in the
Tempered passion
Of her heart.

13.

I only miss you
When my heart beats.
Every breath in
Is a reminder that
We share the same sky,
And every step
Shared earth.

Living for myself
Makes sense;
Living for you
Is purpose.

Aching for you
Is hope.

14.

I'm afraid
That being with you
Has made me
Comfortable
Being alone.

15.

The first to hold me,
And first to understand;
You told our Parents
My name came to you
In a dream.

You've known me
Better than
Most,
But with your
Eyes full of angels
And your
Head full of ghosts,
How can you
See anything else at all?

I've watched
As the
Institution
Peels you away,
Anything recognizable,
And leaves a
Pillar of salt
In the place of someone
I used to know.

I've always been honest,
And I know
You have been too.
But if your truths
Are lies,
Are they truths at all?

I don't believe in truths,
Which,
Truthfully,
Isn't any better.

16.

When you died
I was in awe that
The sun
Continued its rise,
The bees
Continued to visit flowers,
And
My God,
How is it possible that
My heart
Continues to beat?

The reality is that
Somehow
The world goes on
Without you.
The unromantic miracle
Of
Work schedules,
Past due bills,
And
Backyard barbecues
Continuing to exist
Proves that
One day
I may smile again.

Slowly,
Without notice
My
Every second
Thoughts of you
Will be replaced

By
Other people,
Joys,
And worries.
And
Every so often
I will
Savor the pain
That memory brings.

17.

I.

She sat
Above the smoke,
The music,
The laughter;
Beautiful
And dejected.
The sounds of
Black and white
The only response
To her
Melancholy
Song.

A battle
Never won;
Finally lost
In the
Cold bed of a friend.

         Over thought
and under Dosed.

II.

He stood
Beneath the chorus.
Reaching up
To touch
Fleeting fingers.

To him

The heavy,
Unseen,
Mask of karma
Only added
To the beauty of
Her face.

Tables turned;
Petards hoisted;
A taste
Of
Bitter medicine.

III.

Her hair
Was different;
But his fate
Would
Be the same.

Only
A shadow
To be his
Companion,
Until
Even that
Was gone.

18.

How wonderful
Life is
When you're nearby.

How loathsome
When you're gone.

19.

Apathy never was growth.

And there she stood.
Strong, yet unsure.
Poised, yet broken.
Blazing, yet dulled.

She was confusion
Turned steadfast.

Anger
Turned rebellion;
Rebellion
Turned curious;
Curious
Turned brilliance.

Apathy never was strength.
And yet...

"Make me small,"
She said;

"Hold me,
In this tiny place.
Show me
A grand insignificance.
The deep
Exhaled
Suffocation...
Head and heart unseen;

And tomorrow

I can bloom again."

Apathy never was weakness.

20.

We met in a crowded cafe;
I was writing my book
And you were building your thesis.
All the awkward questions with awkward answers;
You said you loved flowers.

17 years later,
It was small at first
Just a stutter,
Stumbling over your words
When you were frustrated;
Forgetting where you'd put your keys
(I do that too);
Then
You forgot the dog's name;
Got upset
That we were out of peanut butter
(You're allergic);
And that time
You were brought home
For driving 10 miles per hour
On the freeway.

We decided to ask the
Impossible question
Knowing any
Response
Wouldn't actually answer..
Words and phrases like

"Early onset"
"Inoperable"
"Inevitable decline"

Have become a customary livable hell.

I lie, eyes wide, terrified that you'll wake and lose your way,
It's happened once before.
You're just as much a stranger to me now
As I am to you.
You threw away the flowers
I placed next to the bed.

I'm standing here, above you.
This place, like my body,
Filled to the brim
Un-moving and writhing.

Placing living things on cold stone in an
Unspoken plea,
I lie down
And turn to grass.

21.

Each passing thought
Of you
Is a
Hot knife
Thrust into this
Wintered heart.

22.

I never did have great timing.

The less time I have
The further I stray
From
Becoming expert.
So how could i ask
That you lose yours
On me?

Thin
                                              gs
don't have
                   To line
                                           Up
Perf
                             ectly...

Do they?

I just
Want to
Spend my
Days,
Count my
Minutes,
Fill my
Mind...
With you.

But the timing isn't right.

I can't

Waste your
Days,
Subtract your
Minutes,
Distract your
Mind...
With me.

And
Anyway...

I never did have great timing.

23.

I can still remember
That feeling of
Watching you from across the room,
Wearing nothing but sunlight,
And
Your teeth still
Etched into my skin.

We were
Two broken pieces
Of the same
Exploded star-planet,
Brought back together
And bound by
The golden cords
Of
Lust and misery.

Who knew
We had so little time?

24.

I hate
That you're gone.

But you wanted to leave,
And we knew you'd leave
From the start.

How can I accept
An absence
I knew
Would happen?

Finding
Anyone
To accept
What I am

Is impossible.

Accepting
Anyone
As they are

Is improbable.

How do I find anyone
But you?

25.

With each passing
Moment
You are away,
I start to write
New beginnings.
Words build
To paragraphs and pages;
Chapters and volumes.

To hear your voice
Rips it all to shreds,
And I am left
Forlorn
With an incomprehensible
Mound
Of
Black ink
And
White paper.

In a
Mad panic
I cannot catch my breath
And
I cannot feel my hands
As I strive
To repair the little work I've done.

I can only
Numb myself
To sleep,
Begin again,
And pray

That the morning dew
Brings no reminder of your tears.

26.

The unquenchable
Dark.
The fear
And freedom
Mixed
To an
Indescribable
Ecstasy.

The impossible
Weight
Of your
Head
On my chest.

No thought
To the
Empty,
Sweet,
Nothings.

You said
You were
Falling.

But why would you be?
With no
Desire
To be caught.

I wish
My monsters
Were

Under
My bed.

27.

Why are you looking at me like that?

A strange distance
In your eyes;
In the past
We would
Gaze at each other in
Quiet awe.
Once so radiant,
Dulled
By the fog of hurt
And
Brimming with sorrow.

A quiver
To your lips;
Once beaming,
We would
Confer in intense
Passion plays
About nothing
Until
We heard the
Sounds of
Dayspring.
Once so bright,
Stony
With no reason
For upturn.

Your brow
Furrowed in
Confused melancholy;

Once raised
In uninhibited rapture,
Ruining sheets
And
Forgetting time.
Once full of wonder,
Heavy
And
Unfamiliar.

I've apologized
So many times,
The phrase
Feels like a forgery
Even to me.

I hate you
Feeling this way;
Why have I become the
Wellspring
Of your
Heartache?

Maybe I'm
Confused and wounded.
Maybe it's
Something you did,
Maybe
Some repressed experience in school,
Maybe
I hate my mother.
Maybe
I just want to ache
And
Cause suffering
Just for the sake of chaos.

But,
Why are you looking at me like that?

28.

Her mouth
Was full of honey,
And her
Body buzzing.
She was a
Swarm of desire
Searching for wildflowers;

But
Honeycomb hangs
From
Branch and corpse
Alike -

And I cannot
Endure
The
Sweet sting
Of conceit
Any longer.

29.

It's only been 10 years,
Why can't I recall your face?

I remember
The night we met,
Affixed
From
Across the room;
I remember
Countless days
And
Innumerable nights
Spent in
Private burial plots,
Cold tombs
Warmed by
Burning hearts.

I remember
The softness
Of your ghostly skin,
And
The sadness
In your sunset eyes.

I must convince myself
Not to look at
Pictures of you,
For fear that
A glance would remind me
Of my
Shallow judgements
And

Cruel words
That sleep with you
In the earth.

30.

I still keep
That picture of us
I found in pieces on the floor,
Strewn amongst
The dried rose petals
From our
Early days of romance.

We look so young
And happy;
Probably less with each other
Than we thought,
And
More in
Anticipation of such a
Vast world ahead of us.

The yellowed tape
Hardly holding
Is a strong reminder
Of
How
It didn't take long
For me to fall out of love
With you.

31.

As if on the back
Of a great snake,
The road opens wide
Its maw
And
I see you nearer to being devoured by its
Endless space
And
Pressing darkness.

I feel I must
Follow,
Whether to
Cut through
Belly and bile
So we both can be free,
Or so that
You are not alone
On your
Journey into the
Abysmal void.

32.

I've been alone.
The focused
Motivation
Of ill contented improvements;
Pondering the future.

I've been in love.
The sweet
Tenderness
Of thinking this will last forever;
No thought outside the now.

I've been obsessed.
The intense
Grasp
Of knowing they are mine;
Sickly rich
And
All encompassing.

And then
There's you.

You remind me
Of how grand
Gritty coffee
And
Shells in scrambled eggs
Are.
Raw cookie dough
And
Spaghetti noodles a bit too thick.

Falling asleep
With one sock on
And the
Magical disarray
Of clothing strewn throughout the house.
The wonder of
A smear of paint on the carpet
And
A pile of
Unfinished masterpieces
Waiting to be remembered.

The significance of
Plastic spoons,
Blemishes
And
Belly button lint.

33.

We won't be here forever,
So let's take the
Lovers leap
And
See what the world
Has to offer.

From the
Volcano of
Mount Mihara,
To Scotland's
Fourth Road Bridge.

Consider Australia's
Gap Cliffs
Or float the
Yangtze river.

Pass through
Prince Edward's
Luminous Veil,
Or perhaps
They've once more
Removed the barriers
On
Grafton.

And then
To end it all,

Fly through
The golden gate
And

Get lost
In the blue
Sea of Trees
Of
Aokigahara.

As long as we
Journey together
The destination
May
Remain a mystery,
And we can join the
Doornails
On the other side of green.

34.

I no longer see you in the morning.
No more your fingers
Running down my spine;
No more your arms
Around my waist;
No more your eyes
Peering into mine;
No more your music
Coming from the next room;
No more your lips
Pressed against my neck;
No more your hair
Glowing in the sun;
No more your voice
Whispering my name;
No more your hushed grace
Making my house a home;
No more your clothes
Scattered across my floor;

Only
Meager remembrance,
Wistful memories,
And
An evocation of still quiet...
A
Disheartened unrest.

No more your presence
In this life.

35.

The amount of times
I have
Loved and lost
By holding myself back
Because of
Superfluous things,
Is too many.

So
I'm going to love you
The way that you are,
As hard as I do,

No matter
The
Distance or time,
Until you tire
Of
Me,
And I grow cold.

And
Even then,
My corpse
Will remember you still.

36.

Winters arrival
Always reminds me of
Alaska.
Simpler times
Of
Long dark nights
And
A backyard full of wildberries.

Surrounded by
Mountains and glacier,
Tucked in
Valleys filled with
Fireweed and devils club,
Flaking birch,
And
Evergreens;

Every town was lush with
Native reminders
Of why we
Loved the nature around us,
And
Dogmatic choices
Seemed irrelevant to
Who we really were.

Moving to a city
Full of great and spacious buildings
Which were, in turn
Filled with
Godly people of worldly ideals
Was an alien landscape

Of
Dried out river beds
And
Rattlesnakes;
All we had was the
Venomous fang
Of
Ill planned experience
As a
Vehicle for escape.

Friends and lovers,
All gone now
In some way
Or another,
Found their way
To
Their own
Cool paradise.

And when I see that
First fall of snow,
Sometimes I think I glimpse
Dancing greens and blues
In the northern sky,
And
A hint of
Purple
Forget-me-nots

Invisible to everyone
But me.

37.

One thing
I know for sure
Is that
I love you.

And
I love me,
Even if
Sometimes I forget.

And us?
I adore us.

38.

When I say I love you
I see the dark.
Your bright silhouette
The only focus.

I find myself crying
In a bathroom
As the music pounds
To the rhythm
Of the thrusts
Of two men
One stall over.

Hand over mouth,
I stifle my sobs
And emerge
Only to find you waiting,
Unaware.

I return to my stall.

When you say you love me
I'm at the top of a list.
Grateful as i am
For your admiration,
It's not the same
Honest words;
There is no comparison.

You cannot understand the
Focused pain,
The earnest anguish,
The desired loss.

I think too much,
And you too little.

You wonder too much,
And I...

39.

My true
Destroyer
Has been keeping myself
Absent
While pining
For an imagined future;

We create these other words for it,
But we know what it is.

On the town
You and I;
Talking
About "us";
How wonderful it is
To have someone really
Know you,
For you...
And then you spoke of a wall.
No distant stronger love
Or
Unresolved discontent.
Just immense fear
Of being blocked
And locked away.

Through bared teeth,
I lied
 And said it was ok.

Pictures
Carefully taken
While the meal grows cold.

Holding
This door open
Is getting
Exhausting.

40.

I am so tired.
So why can't I sleep?

Perhaps I've discovered
The secret
To stopping the passage of time.
If I don't fall to slumber
Days cannot pass,
And
Maybe you won't grow old.
It could be
That I'll never have to witness the
Inevitable stiffened gray.

I can smash all the clocks
To free the birds within,
And you and I will lay here forever,
Never shutting tired eyes
So I can continue
Watching you dream.

41.

You are my waking thought
And my
Afternoon comfort.

A captivating distraction
From thoughts
That would otherwise
Consume me.

I can't help but
Cling
To your presence in my mind
However unaware
You are of me.

The solemn nod
And torturous realization
Of
Empty beds
And
Sleepless nights
Yet to come,
Are almost a small comfort
Wrought with the familiar
Coup de grace.

I try to remember the last time
I was filled with this amount of
Horror
Over things working out in my favor,

And I drown
Beneath the thick depths of

Regret
And
Pleasure.

42.

I want to know
All of the smallest
Things about you;
What's your favorite color?
How do you take your coffee?
Chocolate or vanilla?

I want to watch
Your favorite movie together,
And have you
Talk through the whole thing
To tell me when your
Favorite parts are coming up.

Show me
Something that would seem
Meaningless to anyone else,
But holds your
Dearest memories.
Tell me
How the world has
Changed you,
And
About the friends
You've lost along the way;

What is your place
In the universe,
And
Tell me…

Am I there too?

43.

On a night
Like any other,
Having a drink after work,
Out of the corner of my eye
I noticed you
Laughing with your friends.
You looked so
Unnaturally beautiful,
How could anyone around you
See your smile
And not
Attempt to shield
Their eyes
From the light?

Somehow
I found myself
3 months later,
Waking up to you in my arms,
Your morning glory eyes
And
Cherry blossom lips
Silently telling me
You feel this way too.
We were the
Moon and stars,
Spark to a match,
Shock and awe.

You knew just how
To pull me up
Out of myself
Because

If this pure creature,
This flawless embodiment
Of
Grace,
Was willing to
Shine on this
Darkness....
Willing to
Spend her glow
On me...
Then I must have some
Goodness
Within me.
Weak as I am,
You made me strong.

Why would I leave you?
Why
Did I ever
Leave you?

And now
You're gone.
That brilliance
Dimmed by life and lovers
Until
It was snuffed out completely,
No more light
In this world.
And
As the darkness
Bears down upon me,
My eyes go black,
And I see every mistake
I have ever made,
And how I could have been better.

But
Life is not made up
Of second chances;
And
Death cares not
For regret.

44.

I was thinking of you
And it made me smile..

Your voice is champagne
And
I am drunk on your
Whisper;
Your eyes
Are the light
I see at the end of the tunnel;
Your step
Is water
And I am a barren wasteland,
Thirsting for growth.

I haven't met you
Yet,
But I wonder
If you think of me
And smile too.

45.

You were the first;
The crack in the dam
And the hand turning the
Valves in my brain.
The tsunami of words
Overtook me.

"Drown us,"
You said.
"I never wish carelessly."

But I think you did.
Happy obsession
And
Disoriented attachment
Washed over and
Took my breath away.

So
Thank you,
But
You can't have
My
Poems any more.

46.

Love is not
Happy
Nor
Sad,
But somewhere
In-between.

That
Bittersweet ambivalence
Knowing
Nothing lasts forever.

Hatred,
Isolation
And
Disgust

*"How can a man of consciousness
have the slightest respect for himself?"*

- Fyodor Dostoevsky

47.

The biggest
Change
You can make in the world
Is to
Remove yourself
From it.

48.

The first time,
The anchor
Didn't hold.
I fell to the floor
In a
Crumpled pile
Of waste,
And
Didn't care enough
To find something
More secure.

The second attempt,
I woke
9 hours later;
Cleaned the vomit
From the couch,
Walked the dog,
And crawled into the bedroom -
I fell asleep on the floor.

I was sick for weeks
And
Didn't tell anyone why.

All the
Almosts
In between
Are why I don't
Own
Anything with a trigger.

A failed attempt

A success.
A successful try
A failure.

How many times will I be
Lucky enough to fail?

49.

"Do you think this branch will hold my weight?"
He asked.
The tree bent and cracked
Under the pressure.
Laughter.
A friendly
Insult,
Or two.

It rained that night;
Bough cracking once more,
And an audible snap.
No reprieve
From self
Sentenced
Retribution.

Knees green and red;
Lavender skin
And
Ruby eyes,
Contemplating
The
Unseen sunrise.

The sour smell
Of
Leather and brass.

And we,
Like the tree,
Left
With a heavy

Weight
To bare.

50.

When I'm gone
Know
That I am no longer
Confused and trapped;
My mind has been
Given freedom
Neither sweet,
Nor bitter
For we don't
Contemplate emptiness.

Know
That there was
No way to save me;
I solemnly entered the pit
Long ago.

Know
That my
Internal suffering
Has come to an end.

I could never sleep;
That grinning hag,
Pressure on my chest
And
Withered hands around my throat,
Has withdrawn into the dark.
And now
I rest.

Bury me in an
Unmarked grave;

In an
Unceremonious
Display of how I lived.

Forget me,
And
Let my memory
Fade into
Historical nothingness;

Unfit even for those
Who would
Eat the dead.

51.

I
Don't mind
Your opinion of me.
The
Raging monster
Or
Foolish dolt
That you think I am.

This picture of me
You've assembled,
Using pieces of yourself -
An
Arrogant inhuman thing,
Not worth the effort of a farewell.
A
Tiresome bore,
Meant to
Corrode in quiet despair.
A
Pathetic broken wreck.

I don't mind it,
But
I hate that you believe it.

I hate that you may be right.

52.

Somewhere,
Sunk deep
In the
Caverns of my mind,
An
Incessant haunting melody
Joins the chorus
Of
Shame and regret.

This earworm
With your voice
Has burrowed deep;
Reminds me
Of
Irreparable mistakes
And
Selfish iniquity.

The fruitless attempt
To soften this stone
So the
Gilded lily
May thrive.

I accept who I am,
But not
What I've done;
And
Because the dead cannot hate,
I must join the flagellants
And
Take that mantle

Upon myself
Until
My body decays,
And my memory rots within it.

53.

Grief
Is different for everyone.

Fearing the worst in war;
The surprise of a crashed car;
The expected sadness of
Sickness,
Or old age.

But for those of us
Who lost
To suicide
It is endless,
Knowing
They had a choice.

54.

I drag this weight,
Untethered
But secured,
Over cracked clay
And
Deep mire.

Winged maggots
Above and below
Salivate
In anticipation
Of a repast
Losing its warmth.

Stomach full of coal;
A ring
Burned around the
Throat.
Pressure on the
Wrist,
And
A taste of
Rust
On the tongue.

For this being the only option,
There are so many
Branches
To consider.

55.

I must force myself
To keep
Climbing my way
Up this rope
And out of this
Dry well
Of
Misery,
For I am
Terrified
Of that knot I've tied
At the bottom.

I cannot be the one
Who takes
My mother's son
Away from her.

56.

Yes I know that he wronged you.
Tonight of all nights
Was supposed to be
One
Rare
Happy
Memory.

And now,
It lies in tatters
To be a core
Reminder
Of the
Evil of man.

And
Here you are
To bargain
With the devil himself
For power
Strength
And revenge.

But you must understand,
He is already terrified
Of you.
The
Feminine force
That every woman holds.
The leaves of
Bigoted injustice
Sprout from
The seed of

Fearful insignificance.

Though it may be
A
Cold comfort,
Know that
Change is impending;
That's why they fight so hard.

The shield of power
Is beginning to crack,
And the
Raging terror
Pierces
To their bones.

57.

I just want someone to notice
That I'm slowly killing myself,
And care enough
To stop me.

58.

36 stories down.
6 feet deep in thought.
Mirrored windows,
Twisted faces;
Blurred
By the horror
And speed of it all.

A
Sea of forget me nots
And
Fireweed;
Songbirds
In the dark;
Grave rubbings
And a broken wrist.

The grass had never looked so green;
The stone had never been so gray.

A
Half dream
Of keening sirens
And
Flashing lights.
The drone
Of those
Desperate,
Yet Unable.

The familiar smell
Of chemicals and plastic.

And a frigid hand
Held,
Impossible to warm.

59.

I suppose
Someone
Had to take on
The sickness
That took you from us.

I fear I may have become
The vessel
For this
Incurable cancer;

With crooked fingers
It pushes
Sliver after sliver
Of glassy sorrow
Behind my eyes,
Until my skull
Cracks,
And releases this
Insomniac's nightmare
Upon the world.

60.

It used to be
Massive lows
And
Incredible highs.
I cut myself
In half
And knew exactly what it was
I despised about my existence.

Something happened.

Now it's a
Constant,
Low,
Hum.

And
From my rotted body
Scars continue to blossom,
Until I am enveloped
In the ropes
Of loss
And
Remorse.

61.

With my
Mind in shadow,
And
My eyes
Bleeding salt,
I can see
This sickness
Slowly spread;
Unhappy as it is,
It will not be content
Until
Oil spill tendrils
Hook us all.

I have no doubt
My voice
Will inevitably
Join the
Shrieking symphony
That is this world,
As a reminder
That we are not alone
In our solitude.

I truly hope
That one day,
Albeit after my time
Has come to an end,
Some comforting glint of light
Can penetrate
This murky shell
That presses us to the ground
And forces itself inside us;

Though I fear
Too many
View goodness
As weakness.
And too many
Will lose their private battle,
Unable to forge on
To war.

62.

The chaos grew.
He had stooped so low,
But
Even a crawl
Was still above her head.

Craving something,
Anything,
Different;
He remembered
The sweet
Smell
Of gasoline.

Family road trips.
Warm summer drives.

Shivering;
Frozen,
From the
Rose colored view
Being smeared
Black and blind.

The
Painful first
Thrust
To a
Perfect
Euphoria.

The
Painful last
Blazing

Steps.

Finally warm again.
Embraced.
Going the way
Only monks
And angels do.

63.

There's no way to tell what's going on
When everyone around you
Can't stand to overwhelm you.

Seemingly trapped upstairs
And feeling the
Heat of disdain
Seep through the floor;
You pick up the overturned chair,
Clean up the scraps of hawser,
And move to the open window.

They'll never know
What you took from them,
And somehow
That makes it harder.

Feeling the
Sticks and stones
On open palms
And
Tender arches,
The haphazard shelter
You carry with yourself
Is starting to crumble into
A trail of
Rotten breadcrumbs
Leading to nowhere.

More people see you now than ever before,
Cold and hollow.
They imagine a story for you;
Something vile
And deserving.

It makes them ok with you
Existing.
But there isn't enough change in the world.

Your shivering solitude
Amongst the sea of
Sickened bodies
Is accompanied only by the
Click of passing heels,
Roaring engines,
Rushing tires,
And a distant siren that only
Flirts assistance.

Your mind begins to quiet,
The shivering slows,
And you finally remember your name.

64.

I miss the days
When disappointment
Was going to bed early.
When heartache
Was cleaning my room.
When grief
Was my dad leaving for work.
When pain
Was scraping my knee.

When regret
Was writing on the wall.

65.

There is so much sadness
And
Turmoil
Brought on by
Uncommunicated thoughts
And
Unspoken passions.

If only
We were aware
Of
The winding,
Complex intent
Behind human actions,
Unforeseen beginnings
Filled with bright spirits
Would fall upon us;
And
Endings would come
On time,
With a solemn understanding.

It seems
That the fear of being
Misunderstood,
Keeps us
Outside of each others
Grasp,
Doomed to endure
A
Haunting
Uncertainty.

66.

His heart had become heavy,
Blackened by
Sacramental
Cinder and ash
And
A great weight on his
soul.

Don the sackcloth
And
Accept the
Black goat.
Cover his skin
In desolation and ruin.
His repentance
Will be
Long and severe;
Shrieking regret
And
Gnashing blackened teeth.

May there be a change
To his inward condition.

May he emerge
Forever debased.

May he find
That amongst all the
Disaster and unbearable doubt

We can find comfort
In death.

67.

The only way
I could ever
Hope to win this race,
Is if I was the only
Rat
In this mischief.

If I was the one
To sound off
The starting gun
I just may have had a chance
To finish with dignity
And
Some sort of self respect,
Though
I fear the only trigger I pull
May signify the end;

The
Wasted steps
Of a
Slow sprint.

68.

I was born in this house.

I've gone through
Deep seeded
Times of wanting to leave,
But
It's always
Questions of
"Where would I go?"
And
Pictures of
My mother
Getting woken from
Her sleep
Being told that
I'm gone.

I stare out of dark windows
Onto
Buzzing grasslands,
That seem to be filled with
Bright living objects;

And
Every once in a while,
I invite one
To stay a while.
But they inevitably
Tire
Of sorting through
The staggered piles
Of collected
Nonsense
I've amassed over the years.

The weight of it crushes me too.

69.

We used to own snakes.
Feeding day was always exciting.
New friends
Would come over to watch;
Some spellbound and sober,
Most
Celebrating in an
Intoxicated exhilaration.

You can't put
The food
In and simply watch.
You have to prepare it first;
Snap the rabbits neck
So it doesn't
Try to defend itself
And go for the soft parts.

The sound they make
When you do it wrong...
It makes
Everything inside of you
Crumple
And force itself between your
Shoulder blades.

And then you have to try again.

I remember
The irony of
A house full of animals,
Some
Significantly alive,
Some meant for death,

And some
Already bones.

The only difference
Between
"Pet" and "Dinner"
Is that some have names.

And I feel
That blow to the back of my head,
That splintered crack,
When someone can't remember
What I'm called.

What would they feed me to?

70.

I am immersed
In the
Thick depths
Of despair;
Heavy waves of
Hopeless apathy
Crash somewhere above me,
And
I am too weary
To try to reach the surface.

71.

I keep asking myself for something,
But I look down
To see empty hands

Why must I
Force myself
To take care of
This body
That refuses
To return the favor?

I was once
Living kindling,
Keeping someone warm;
Now
Burnt up,
Cold and useless -

I suppose
Fine arts have been
Composed
In charcoal,
But isn't it
Someone else's
Hands
That brings us to life?

I long to be
Smeared across
A blank page until
My abstract chaos
Becomes
An artists

Magnum opus.

I keep asking myself for something,
And I look down,
To see no hands at all.

72.

There are people out there,
Many
Many
People,
Who will say they have the answers.
I don't know,
But what I've learned
Is that
Anyone who claims to know the truth
Is wrong.

That's the only thing
That makes any sense at all.

"To err is human.."
Right?
How could we ever understand
The divine?
Even if one of us,
Writhing and small,
Saw the
Truth of it all...
Could we comprehend
Through our calloused eyes
And impenitent minds?
Could we
Describe it,
"The meaning",
Using the handful of useless words
Amongst finite language
And
Callow understanding?

If
It is true...
All the
Saints and stigmata,
The
Collars and crosses,
The
Wafers and wine,
The
Seer stones and censers,
The
Murti and martyrs,
The
Hell and holy water,
The
Sacrament and Satan,
The
Paraments and pulpits,
The
Faith and flagellants,
The
Rituals and rosary,
The
Crowns and cowls,
The
Baptism and blood,
The
Zen and Zion,
The,
Rabbis and resurrections,
The
Secrets and symbols,
The
Hymns and hate;

What would be the difference?

The world would
Crumble still,
And we within it,
Only to be tossed into the
Landfill
That is the
Void of space.

73.

I exist without being seen;
I know I can
See and hear
What you
Do and say,
But I can't be sure that I'm not the one
Acting and speaking.

I put so much value
On these
Rare little creatures.

I pretend that they are
Either
Better than
Or
Lesser than
Myself and each other.
For my own
Pitiful sake,
I secretly hope you are all
Inferior to me,
Although I end up
In the middle of my own
Moral list.

I've got to get out of this body;
Though I cannot say
Where my mind ends,
And my fingers begin.
I do know that I peer into the same
Reflection every morning,
Even when it doesn't smile back.

I can say with surety
That my body is the vat
My brain dwells in -
I am the evil demon
Creating my own
Falsely perceived
Flesh and blood.

I am left frantic
Accepting finite,
And staggered
Accepting infinite,
Leaving me with the
Immense weight
Of
Innumerable
Options between.

The solipsistic fear
Cannot be undone,
And I
Wonder
How long I can
Stomach
This
Private
Frenzy.

74.

Glued to a corner,
Finger on the trigger.
Forcing my feet
To carry me to the other side;
I failed the numerary,
So
I know this
Perpetual feeling
Of dread,
Something undone,
Will always follow,
At least
Until
I forget...
Three
By
Three.

Stop.

.Vixi.
I lived.

Stop.

75.

Why do we
Convince children
Of
So many lies?

What a strange irony
That
I was taught free will
Was the core of my belief;

How can you
Go astray
If we're here
On our own volition?

There is
No sin,
No commandment,
No principle,
No creed,
No judgment,
No punishment,
No hell.

That is to say,
There is
No virtue,
No invocation,
No gospel,
No truth,
No sense,
No reward,
No heaven.

I resist
These
Lavish lies,
Woven by
Scared dead men
In the
Ornate darkness
Of
Perceived power.

I am the adversary,
And
I am called
Honesty.

76.

I watched
And was aware
When he wouldn't shake a gay
Man's hand.
This person I viewed as so strong,
Smart,
Witty,
Loving.
Turned fearful,
Oblivious,
Grave,
Bitter;
Afraid of a touch.

That night
He took me on a drive
In his truck,
And asked me
If I was gay.
Why would I say yes?

77.

A voice said:
"No one cares
About the
Unhinged turmoil.
You are much too heavy
A burden."

No
Jaw or timbre,
Only
Bony fingers
That
Uncurl in my brain
To
Stab and
Stab and
Stab and
Stab and
Stab.

It is a
Low rumble
In my blood;
A
Splintering havoc
In the bowels
Of my mind.

Solid ground is snatched away
And I fall
Into
Dark delirium
Unable to determine

Which course
Will lead me
To hope,
And which
Will lead me
To
Burn it all to the ground
In a show of
Malicious desecration.

78.

I don't miss you,
But saying you didn't want to
Be around me
Made me search the
Endless list
Of
Reasons
I can't stand me.

Every doubt became proven,
Every uncertainty confirmed;
When once
You were the calm
To quiet those thoughts.

I don't miss you,
But I feel
Repulsive
Again.

79.

The
Lush
Growth of
Bodily decay
Is mesmerizing.

The abundance of
Writhing life
Within a corpse
Is an inspiring
Community;
The unwashed masses
Festering in a
Swollen universe
Destined to expand until it
Collapses in on itself.

We are like them,
Parasites in a
Rotten world;
Surrounded by
Arrogant maggots
Eating away at everything
Until we sprout wings
And
Move on
To
Swarm over
Bigger and better
Dung heaps,

And finally
Lay our heads down

In the
Night soil.

80.

I'm suffocating.
I look down
Only to see
My own hand
On my throat;
A
Flame on my fingertips
And
Glass in my palms.

Through the calm,
A thick disquiet
Wells from my breast,
Until
My lungs shatter
And my
Body collapses
Under the gravity of
Incipient change.

I
Cannot continue this
Gasping calm,
Choking on relief;

Fighting for air.

I must
Fill my chest with the
Cold wet
Truth
In the marrow of my psyche,

Or otherwise
Drown.

81.

I feel so low
But high spirits
Don't sit
In the safest roost.

A target on my back
And
Crosshairs on my wrist;

Rock bottom
Is hitting me,
And
I don't have the strength
To
Fight back.

82.

Heatless flames,
And a
Broken heart.

Death's womb
Weaving breaths
Hot with
Sickness and decay.

Face devoured by cellophane;
Throat wrapped in leather;
Eyes encased in wax,
Bathed in thunder.

Left alone
For so long
That being apart of
This world
No longer made
Any sense at all.

83.

We walk
In an endless spiral,
Dictated by chance
No matter
The amount of
Effort,
Thought,
Or planning
We feel we
Use.

Control is a fraud;
A
Feigned attempt
At comfort
In an
Unbearable world.

I cannot believe
That at the
Conclusion
Of this
Tired game
We move on in an
Infinite existence.
Never ceasing,
Spiritless
And
Broken.

So don't.

The closer you get,

The further away I'll seem.
Chancing a touch,
I fear I may
Penetrate your mind
And
Pollute everything you know.
Pull you apart
And
Eat away what you're made of.

Don't.

I fear you'll be
Whisked away into the
Ebon void
Of my
Totality.

84.

I get
Creative when I'm
Alone.
I begin working on myself,
Art,
Pastimes.

I am
Happy when I have a
Partner.
I become motivated,
Social,
Excited.

But,
When I'm somewhere in between…
When I'm not sure
What this
Empty limbo is…
Overflowing with
Insecurity until
Doubt runs from my eyes
And I am
Soaked in ache and
Uncertainty..
I only
Dwell on whether I should
Sit or stand;
Maybe if I run fast enough
I can leave this panic
Behind.
Or sleep
Until I wake

Into a new,
More sure,
Reality.

85.

Please no more
Of
This dreaded sun.
It is an
Unfamiliar warmth
That makes my
Skin crawl.

Please, one more
Night;
A
Shaking body,
Empty eyes,
And
Stiff fingers
Strangle my past,
My present,
And
My future.

Please, it's more
Than I can stand
To drown under
Wave after wave
Of memories;
Useless
20/20
Blinding my view
Of tomorrow.

Cold hands
Lead to
Thickened blood

And
A still heart.

86.

It's always
Too old
Too young
Too ugly
Too emotional
Too vague
Too awkward
Too much..

Too me.

Not enough.

Really,
I'm aware that logically
Things don't go as we plan them;
Statistically
Failure is inevitable;
Realistically
Things will
"Work out in due time."

Logic
Always
Has its
Downfalls.

I need an
Illogical
Person.

87.

I crumble
Into
A mound
Of
Refuse and spoil.

How is it
That you see more
Than this
Insignificant heap?
The torn gauze
I've forced over
Your blind and bleeding
Eyes.

Soon
You'll recognize
That I am a cross to bear,
With no reward of
Martyrdom;
Only a future
Crushed
By the feet of reality.

Blood to wine
And bone to dust,
You will be left
Drunk
Dry
And wanting;
Depleted of all virtue and goodness.
Derelict and decayed.

88.

I hope
Your family dies.
Your dog to be hit by a car,
And
You're in a relationship
With a man who
Manipulates,
Belittles,
And
Beats you.

I'd like
Your mother
To get cancer
And your sister to get
Addicted to heroin;
Your brother
To get a
Young girl pregnant
On a one night stand,
And your father to die at fifty.

If
Only
You could be
Diagnosed
With some sort of
Illness;
Chronic
Or
Terminal,
It doesn't matter.

I wish

For you
To be
Crushed,
Downtrodden,
Turned to a shuddering,
Terrified
Creature.

Because I love you.

And,
Maybe then,
I could look strong
In comparison;
Sick as I am.
Maybe then,
You would fall into my arms,
Exhausted and grateful.

And I could keep you forever.

89.

The spirit
That my body hosts
Is not worthy
Of
Beauty or goodness.

I feel compelled to make them equal.

90.

I can't stand
Too much of the sweet,
I'd rather savor
A little bit of the bitterness.

With opal eyes
And a silver tongue,
I'm drawn
To the nostalgic
Flavor
Of
Complex disappointment
And
Elaborate despair.

I refuse to waste my time
Pursuing the
Honeyed untruth
Of
Blissful ignorance.

91.

We waste so much time
Applying the past
To a
Future we control.

92.

I cannot stop myself
From
Ranting needless advice
To heedless ears.

It must
Clothe some inner
Fear of my own
Spiraling existence;

I've turned bitter
And
Grown deaf
To counsel
Other than my own
Tired
Ego.

In whose arms
Will I finally
Fall,
And rest
Until the end of time?

Under whose feet
Will I
Be crushed
Until I become
One with
This
Polar landscape -

A deep crimson smear

Upon
Stark white cotton.

93.

If I wake one more morning
To this feeling of
Empty despair,

If I float through one more day
With this feeling of
Dulled apathy,

If I crumble into one more sleep
With this feeling of
Hollow isolation;

If I spend one more night
Sick to the back teeth,

I may never attempt 24 hours again.

94.

I don't talk
About my depression
With my family anymore,
Because I learned
Long ago
That they understand all too well;
But they don't
Talk about theirs either.

I know it's hard
For parents to look
Broken
In front of their children,
And
It's so exhausting
Telling those we love
About our
Failures,
Especially when that
Failure
Feels like our entire being;
Past,
Future,
And
Today.

So instead,
We talk about work,
Television,
Dinner,
The weather;
And end the conversation
With a subdued

"I love you"
As an
Acknowledging
Nod
That even if
We don't feel like enough,
We know the other
Is.

95.

Everything is ok.
Those thoughts
Don't get to me anymore.

I've reached a point of
Comfort
With who I am
And who I can become.
I see the value in life,
And
The love that surrounds me.
I will wake up
Knowing
I can face
Whatever
Heartache
Tumbles upon me today.

Everything will be ok.

And
I will continue
These murmured lies
Until
My embittered end.

96.

It is time.

Time for change.
Time for healing.
Time for relief.

If I remain
Buried beneath all this
Ache and solitude
I soon
Will become
Forever lost
Amongst the damned.

I will
Claw through mud and filth
With broken hands,
Pull myself out of
This tomb,
And
Live again.

Unseen
Horrors
And
Unknown
Realities

*"When he has lost all hope,
all object in life, man becomes
a monster in his misery."*

-Fyodor Dostoevsky

97.

She was so young.

Her body
Was
Slumped
In such a way
That you would swear
She was dreaming;

White dress
Bathed in red,
Her breast seemed to
Rise and fall
With the rhythm of
The waves
Near the ocean rocks
She was
Found on.

His body
Was nearer the water,
A smile on his face,
And
Grimace on his wrist,
Fingers still
Tightly grasping
The blade.

37 times
He had thrust inside of her,
Each time
Creating a new
Open window view

Into her
Heart and soul.

What
Last thoughts
Had
Flooded her mind,
And where
Had he
Taken them?

She was so young…
And,
Though headless as she was,
You could see
That
She had been beautiful.

98.

The plate
That I feed from
Is
Brimming with hunger.

These sinuous
Nightmares
Overflow
Into reality
And
I cannot tell the difference
Between
Morning and night,
Slumber and wake,
Pleasure and despair.

I attempt to walk,
Maybe navigate some other
Horrid reality,
Different all the same,
Only to realize
My legs have been
Mislaid.

Seeing no immediate threat,
Doesn't mean it isn't there;
Only that the
Arachnoid membrane
May be too thick;
The cowl
Too low.

My heart has

Turned to bone.
You are out of this world.

99.

Black streets
Still wet from the rain
Hours before,
Streetlights
Above and below
Reflected in
Still puddles,
And the lonely fall
Of
Her footsteps
Passing
Empty alleyways.
She knows the dangers
That live in the shadows
Of
The city,
But home is so close;
Inhibitions so far.

She senses another body
Far behind,
Hears the
Thud of boots
And
Heavy breaths
As
Thick arms
Wrap around her waist.

There's an odor of desperation and yearning.
When she turns
There is no face,
Only burning eyes

Accustomed to taking what they see.

Torn cloth,
And a jingle of coins
Hitting the sidewalk.
Terror begins to build.
Her head hits the pavement,
Her face flushes hot;
And she smiles,
Showing
Blood smeared teeth.

Her smile
And his eyes
Grow wide,
Until the stretch of flesh can no longer
Take the strain.
Transference of fear
And
Power;
A toppled table;
The sky shatters
To reveal
A weird irony,
And a lesson learned too late.

He tries to escape,
Leaving
Broken nails in sidewalk cracks.
Crumpled lungs
Hiss and whine,
Like a puling infant.

She
Unhinges
Her jaw,

And
Goes for the throat.

100.

I.

The world as I knew it
Is gone;
Only a
Dystopian nightmare
Remains.

I know there are others,
Survivors -
They live because they were
Weak.
The self contained,
Fearful,
Cowards.
We found dark spaces,
Small,
Lonely,
And quiet.

We once had companions,
Families, maybe.
We tried to live;
Scavenge,
Collect,
Fight,
Start over...
Like we saw in the movies.

But in the end,
If we didn't eat each other,
It found us.

II.

The crickets have ceased their
Incessant screams.
I know
That
Thing
Is out there.

The aberrant figure
Full of
Blind eyes
And
Gnashing gums;
It only seeks to
Feed,
Though it shows no sign of
Being nourished.

The foul shape,
Vile and twisted;
It leaves a trail of
Unknown seepage
And rot,
Its only sound
A low
Cacophony of
Croaking whispers
And struggled chokes
On phlegm and gall.

It knows
I'm here.

If I try to run
I will be caught.

III.

While it may be the
Easy way,
The cold taste of steel is comforting.
And with a twitch of a finger
I leave behind
A masterpiece Pollock would be proud of.
My last thought is of relief
And
Comfort;
Never to run again.

101.

Sleep is broken
By itchy eyes
And
Sandpaper tongue.

He slides his legs,
Heavy and still in
Half slumber,
Across the bed
And to the floor-
The rest of him follows.

It seems
Unusually dark
Tonight,
And
So quiet.
The only sound is
The
Soft slide and thud
Of bare feet
On wood floors
Accompanied by
The house sinking into itself.

He fills his glass;
The low rush of water
Matches the drone of
Roaring blood
In his ears.

As he makes his way back,
A sweet stench of forgotten life fills the air.

The wallpaper comes alive,
Pulsing waves forced
From some
Unseen creatures within,
And the floorboards crawl with
Insects forcing escape
From the bowels of the house.

Stumbling into the bedchamber,
A frigid cold
Takes over.
A slumped figure lays beneath the sheets,
Misshapen and unmoving...
And
The stab of
Static fear pours over his shoulders.

Drawn out, sluggish steps
Carry him to the side of the bed,
Where he looks into
Empty, familiar eyes
And
A bloated face,
Made up of blues and yellows
That he once only saw in
Reflection.

He considers the pills scattered across the floor,
And
Knows
It will be a long time before someone
Discovers him here.

Struggling to remember
Who he was,
He

Drinks deeply from the cup,
But is left
Thirsting
And
Alone.

102.

I remember the circus was in town.
Bright lights and laughter,
Cotton candy and bells.
The Ferris wheel slowly spinning
In
A whirlwind of
Revelry.

But I was lost.
Where had my mother gone?

My cries and questions
Blended with the
Screams of delight
From passers by.
Every dress
Looks like hers.

I pass from booth to booth,
Happy families
And
Cross eyed
Bears,
Until I find myself
Away from the clamor;
And I think I can
Hear her voice
Say my name.

Outside a tent
All
Red and white,
I pull back the

Canvas doorway,
Heavy
And
Awfully rough on my hands...

And I see her.

Her perfect face
And her makeup
She takes so much pride in
Smeared
And
Tear stained,
Twisted in a
Show of
Pure horror.
Her blouse
She took so much time to press,
Flowers all blue and yellow,
Torn and
Tight around her neck.
Her body
Always so poised and perfect
Held down
By
Gloved hands
And streaked in grease paint.

One of them lifts up
Heavy eyes
To
Meet my own.
The
"Entrance of the Gladiators"
Plays its
Tedious melody,

And
I cannot tell
Whether his smile is
Genuine
Or painted on.

The rest
Laugh
At some
Playful joke
Unknown to me.

I hear
Heavy shoes
And
Smell
Dust and hay
As the world goes black
And my mother's cries
Fade
To a muffled
Whimper…

I cannot help her.
And
I will never go to the circus again.

103.

A planet
Heavy with mourning,
Hung in dross.
Men suck
Cigars
Like mother's tit.

Oh my God,
Hardly seen
Through
The walls of
This cage
I keep her in.

Please
Put your penny
Back in your
Pocket.
I only want
Your
Ears
And
Eyes.

Too late now.
Catch a ride
With
Sisyphus.
This igneous transport
Is
Much too fast
For me;
I'll crawl,

Thank you.

(Stumped to
Shoulder
And
Pelvis,
But still,
A few good
Lashes
Will get me there.)

Are we there yet?
Do we want to be?

Would you mind
Interrupting
me?

I'd like
To gather
Some moss.

104.

I.

A bump in the road.
I awake into nothingness
Bringing life to my thoughts,
With a blinding reminder
Of how much my head hurts.
I'm not sure how I got here,
I can only feel the splintered walls close around me
As I realize I can't extend my legs.

I try to wipe what must be blood
I feel falling down my face,
Only to realize my wrists are caught
By thick and unforgiving
Bonds.

I feel the asphalt
Turn to gravel,
Turn to dirt,
Turn to forest.
The familiar squeal of brakes
Tell me we've arrived.
A car door slams.

Silence.

Then blinding white pain.

II.

I awake once more to black, and bones.

Others have come and gone.
Light shining through the floorboards
And the sound of a body below.
I can hear him eating,
And I wonder what side of the table I may end up on.

Days,
Nights,
Weeks..
Months?
I'm visited all too often
By blurred Fists,
Calloused lips,
And hungry eyes.
Surrounded by chunks of
Hair and flesh
Once mine,
I think of my mother,
And wonder why she never
Wore white in the summer.

How many were here before,
And who will follow?
What will be left of me,
Wretched as I am.

III.

I awake to mourning,
And the creak
Of rotted floorboards
Under the weight of dense leather,
And a crumbled sole.
The flash of copper and the never ending moan
Of hinges that have lost their way,

I know this time is different.
I can smell it.
I choke on the palpable change of intent
Rushing in to overwhelm every crevice of my body.

A pause.
He seems more scared than me.
A smile.
He slides off his belt, and
Puts it around my neck.
I feel it,
Warm and tight
On my throat.
Boot to my chest,
I feel my ribs
Bend and break
And even though it will disappoint,
I forget how to scream.

My mouth fills with
Iron and bile,
Jaw slack,
And one last exhausted exhale.
My limbs sag,
And my body releases my mind.

What horrors will I face now?

105.

No morning...
Never.

Futures
Once realized,
Now
Crushed hopes
And Rotten dreams.

Skeleton willows.
Sinew moss.
Lining the banks
Of
Rivers never meant to run.

Obsidian grasses,
Edges softer
Than the
Touch of some,
Run to the edge of eternity.

Parasitic beasts
Of herculean proportion,
Filled to bursting
With gore;
Mere incubators
For shadowed figures
Within.

The constant
Struggle
To remember
Something lost

And
Forgotten.

No mourning...
Never.

106.

Ritual circles,
A low flame,
And
A pit.
Bone
Wrapped in
Dry leather,
Draped in
Liquid silver,
Obscured within
Pitch-stained cloth
Stinking of
Saffron and iron salt;

Forked tongues
Weave black symbols
To be left
In places unseen.
Your body bleeds
A storm of
Blue and green;
Fill the crown
And
Drain the flask;
Let him fill
Every
Bright corner
Of these remains.

No room for
Dreams,
Only terror and ruin.

The
Blind worm
Feeds on virtue,
And
It will be satisfied.
Every moment after this
Will be devoted to
Its seed,
Until
You are left
Barren,
Used,
And
Hollow.

107.

I.

Escaping the nightmare,
She
Comes back to reality
Drowning in sweat,
Heart still racing
From the fear and
Unseen faces
She knows are
In the dark.

These
Blackened dreams
Have been more
Persistent,
And
The voice...
His voice,
Is becoming more familiar;
Like a
Thick,
Wet,
Blanket of frost.

It started as just a whisper,
Until it was a
Hoarse scream;
And
He introduced himself,
Her new companion
Within.

For no reason at all
The
Anger
Turns to
Rage,
The
Rage
Turns to
Seething,
And the
Seething
Turns to
Hate.

White hot confusion
And
So many hands.
Six fingers all,
Broken nails and
Stiffened articulates,
Grasp her by
Shoulder, hip, and thigh;
Drag her back into the
Sticky core
Of her own
Heart.

And
His name is
Torment.

II.

Emaciated and captive
On a childhood mattress
Now

A blanketed coffin.
This room
Stinks of
Excrement and evil,
Bile and blood ring her cracked lips
That break into a smile
As
Men in collars
Circle like wolves;
They place a cross above her head.

God's love
Is nowhere to be found here,
Though they
Recite His word;
It starts from a
Mumbled hope
And
Grows to a
Shrieking earnest.

No power
And
Uncompelled.

Water burns flesh,
A writhing agony
Of loathing incarnate;
Bonds broken,
Fingers and sole
Leave prints on the ceiling.
Bones ache and bend
Under inhuman strain,
And
Unearthly howls.

Guttural reminders
Of sins long past:
Youthful lust,
Golden avarice,
Unsatiated gluttony,
Self fulfilled pride,
Unseen outrage,
Stolen jealousy,
Hedonistic sloth.

All light
Is sucked into
Nothing.
There is
Nothing left at all.

And
His name is
Agony.

III.

She still
Draws breath,
Somewhere deep
Behind her eyes.
She sees and
Feels
Everything,
But holds no sway.
Lost and
Beaten down,
She only
Retreats further into the gray.
The
Holy war

That exists outside of her,
Caused by a
Battle lost,
Thrives
Until
Countless bodies
Tell the story of a pointless struggle.

He laughs,
Her body quiets,
While her mind still
Weeps.
The very last of her
Is picked away
And
She knows
Through no fault of her own
She will
Stay here forever.

And
His name is
Anguish.

108.

The phone call came late.

I said that I knew the name,
And would come
As quickly as possible.

This bid to arms
Brought me to familiar
Emergency room doors,
And
Though I expected the worst
I was struck with
Chilled horror
As they led me down a hall marked
"Morgue".

Passages,
Elevators,
Too many steps to count,
Lead me and my
Clipboard issued ferryman
To a door
Just like the rest,
But foreboding all the more.
I learn that I've been brought here to identify,
Although I can't tell my
Tongue from my teeth.

A lying figure
Bathed in thin white
Hanging heavy to the ground
Seems poised in
Honored excitement

At my approach.
The slow pulling back of the
Cool shroud
Is a perpetual
Stop motion
Of endless cloth,
And
I start to wonder if I've grown old
In this labored passing of time.

There is nothing about this
Husk
That equates to who she is,
But I acknowledge a
Coffee stain birthmark
I've traced with reverent fingers
A million times
On
Endless tranquil nights
Lifetimes ago.

I leave this building
Housing sick and sorrow,
To be confronted by
Flashing lights
And a
Recitement of rights.
As the car door slams
My sadness and confusion
Unite in an
Epic understanding
That
The last time I really lived
Was when I looked into her eyes,
Just as her with mine.

109.

The sound of leaves
Crunching beneath my feet,
And
The scrape of dirt and gravel
Are accompanied by
The static rattle of
A
Low rush of wind through the trees.

The usual
Scurry of small shapes
Darting into the undergrowth
And
Forest drone
Of
Frogs and insects
Is gone,
And I wonder
If there is room for them
In whatever space they've
Chosen to
Occupy
Instead.

The dark
Seems to dampen my senses
As I trudge this
Gloomy trail
Blind and mute.

The trees grow thicker.

Making my way becomes more difficult

As the trail
Thins and disappears.

Moving bone branches
Stretching
From skeleton trees
My hand catches on
Sticky thread
Draped across the path.
Palm to my face
My focus shifts through open fingers
And I notice
Eight gigantic legs
And feel
A thousand eyes.

A piercing pain.

Turning,
Only to realize I am surrounded by
A tangle of knotted lace -
An intricate network of gluey muck;
Shriveled forms
Hang like rotten fruit,
And I know
I will join them soon.
Raptured by
Pedipalps and claws;
Swaddled in thick white;
Surrounded by
Tombstone tree stumps
And
Grave pit mire.

110.

I stand
Under the warm glow
Of a summer sun,
Surrounded by shining green
And a canopy of fluorescent leaves.
The hum of
Hives and hills
Fills the air,
And
Birds compose letters in the blue.

Before me is a home,
Its door open wide.
And it beckons with
A promise of shelter
And calm respite.

Crossing the threshold,
I'm met with
Cool air
And bare floors.
I hook my fingers around hung drapery
And place my hands against icy glass.
Peering through the pane
I see a blanket of white,
A chilled sparkle covers
Dead branches,
Crooked and quiet.

I turn
To realize this
Chamber is devoid of comfort,
Unfurnished,

Silent and sharp;

July is beyond my grasp
And
I will stay here for far too long.

111.

He stands perched,
One light dead
And
The other blinded
By
Night and foam,
Hate
And
Vengeance.
The open sea
Writhes on
In endless
Rolling hills
Of
White and green,
Black
And
Blue.

The rest of them
Crouch behind,
Each at their post,
Each
Cloaked in
Ink and scars,
Devotion
And
Steel.
Sometimes there are
Fleeting memories
Of
Lives long ago,
Feet sinking in

Moss and soil,
Sand
And
Grass.

Lamps filled with
Oil
And
Pockets full of
Ambergris,
They've seen the signs
Of
Hunted prey
Though it seeks them too;
Calculated and certain,
Hungry
And
Mad.

With a sudden
Shudder
And a
Splintered shriek,
Tendrils slither
All around;
Veins and membrane,
Boneless
And
Unnerving.

Vessel crushed
And
The battle lost
Before it began;
The gargled screams
Of friends and companions,

Crew
And
Boon,
Rush into his head
Blending with thoughts of
A
Life wasted on revenge;
Thoughts of
Fear and remorse,
Terror
And
Dread.

This behemoth
Drags him down;
Descending
Into the murky black,
Engulfed
As the
Last few bubbles
Escape
His lungs
Scurrying
To the surface;

Slow and steady...
Forgotten
And
Lost.

112.

There is so much darkness.
An assault of
Inky gloom
Spilling in
Every endless direction,
Heavy black
Crushing bone
And
Dull needles
Shredding
Soft tissue,
Haphazard and senseless.

Things
That dwell here
Are an
Immense
Bloated mess;
Tumorous
Fat bulges from
Bulky frames,
Cancerous and sick.
Hulking and clumsy
In the distant space...
Bastards, all.

A
Gnarled mass
Of flesh
And fingers;
Too many legs
And
Rigid tiny hands

Clench and relax
Clawing at time,
Searching for anything to
Tear and destroy.

Panic
And
Paralyzed horror
Hangs
Dense in the air.

The blaring silence
Is only
Broken by
Thunder
And the
Violent clangor
Of
Hammered steel;
Seismic aftershock
And
Quivering atmosphere
All around.

Toothy beaks
Pick decay
From
Delicate remains.
Faces missing
Everything
That would
Make them
Recognizably human;
Thick tissue
Grown over
Sightless sockets;

Hollow cheeks
Have become
Windows
To
Blackened tooth
And
Pestilent gum;
Lips devoured
In
Panicked hunger
Long ago,
While starving
Bellies roar
For some
Sort of
Cessation.

These
Somber forms
Hung in
Twisted tapestry.

I
Cannot remember
Who I am
Or
What brought me;
But
This is my
Familiar.
And
I find comfort here.

113.

It's time for you to meet them,
The dark hooded
Circle of
Cultist patriarchs
That are the bruises on your skin.

Take the
Self administered
Communion of blood
And
Try to wash away
The sins of your father.

Leave the congregation
But continue your life
Being baptized in
Adam's ale,
Left with the
Headache
Of
Injustice.

114.

Underexposed
And blind.
Oversensitive
Clouded eyes,
Stimulated
To the point of blister.

Can't ever
Callus
If the
Wound
Doesn't heal.
The sore
Is more
Appalling
Anyway.

You can always
Find
A new
God.

So we
Took
All that we could;
Fused
To
Meat
And
Bone.

Disfigured.

But content.

                    (Never content.)
Removal of
Flesh
To an unrecognizable
Mess.

At least with
Betrayal
You can hold your head high
As you
Masturbate
Into the crowd;
You've so many
Children
To lead.

It pierces to the bone
Only because
I'm choosing
To move.

These bed sores
Are
Getting old.

115.

There once was life.
Now
Infection spreads,
And fills the cavity;
Purulent and distended
Yet devoid of any soul.
The
Seeping should cause relief;
Even so
None to be found.

Joy,
Logic,
Reason,
Future;
All lost.
In their place only
Panic,
Bedlam,
Doubt,
Passing.

Finally clutch the
Infant,
Cold and still,
Smeared and stained.
Still connected with nothing.
Born into agony.

Cut the cord
And bury the frame.

116.

My
Fitful dreams
Are interrupted
By the
Nasty sting of
Sulfur and ash.

Head and heart pounding
And
Eyes still obscured by sleep,
I cannot tell
If this murky haze
Is reality,
Or my mind's continued
Embrace with
Nightmarish stupor.

Dogs barking
And
Children crying,
I realize my all too eminent demise.
The
Panic-stricken
Consideration of lists upon numbers
Of items and memories to save;
The
Split-second
knowledge of
A future without anything I know;
The
Wild-eyed
Search for anything to take hold of.

Flickering lights
And billowing black,
I grab a door handle
I've never particularly considered,
And am left with
Searing pain,
And
Branded tissue
I will know forever.

A splash of embers,
And a
Deafening roar,
But an end to the cries and howls
Tell me it's too late for
Redemption,

My body carries my
Feet over coals anyway,
Through a familiar passage
Once covered in the
Wax musings of youth
Now barren, black, and hot.
I am met with melted polyester,
Glowing cotton,
Candle bedposts,
And a
Curled lump of coal
I once held close to my heart.

I know that down the steps
There is cool air
And exposed sanctuary.
Dragging myself down
An incandescent hall,
My feet

Leave a
Thick trail of
Meat and sorrow.

I cannot see,
I cannot make a sound;
The air is so solid
I am entwined as recrement.

I reach up
Gaunt fingers
on
Trembling hands,
And
Crumble to my knees
As
Flesh slides from bone.

I lean my head back
In a silent
Smoldering
Death rattle,
Enveloped in the
Bright,
Blazing,
Abyss.

117.

The pounding of a hammer
Marrying nails to wood,
The smell of pine,
And my own panicked breaths
Are my only companions.

Tossed to the side,
I feel the familiar tear of flesh.
I focus,
See a neon moon between slats of timber,
And begin to hear the
Slow,
Repetitive,
Scrape
Of shovel and dirt.
It goes on for an eternity,
Tedious and mundane.
Earth moving.

As I feel my forced refuge
Moved from one unknown place
To another,
A dull crash and loss of breath tells me
I now occupy whatever
Depression
That was seemingly created for me.
Again the familiar scrape,
Followed by the sound of
Stone and gravel
Beating down above my head.

The shadowed gloom takes over,
The air grows thick and hot;

My heart races, filling my chest
Until my lungs have no more space to grow.

A cavity filled
In the mouth of the forest,
And muffled screams,
Barely more than a hum,
Dim to silence.

*"This is my last message to you:
in sorrow, seek happiness."*

-Fyodor Dostoevsky

ABOUT THE AUTHOR

McKay Child was born in 1985, and raised in Eagle River, Alaska, before moving to Utah, where he now resides in Salt Lake City. A career Chef, McKay is also a painter, cellist, and avid collector of dead things, and tattoos. When not working in the kitchen, he can be found reading with his all-too faithful black lab, Bone. *6 Feet Deep in Thought* is McKay's first book.

Made in the USA
Monee, IL
10 August 2023

51043c7b-bc85-42cf-9ede-1c454a1b284bR01